SHONEN JUMP'S ONE PIECE

RECIPE FOR DISASTER

Adapted by Michael Anthony Steele

SCHOLASTIC INC.

New York   Toronto   London   Auckland   Sydney
Mexico City   New Delhi   Hong Kong   Buenos Aires

ISBN-13: 978-0-439-89722-8
ISBN-10: 0-439-89722-X

© 2007 Eiichiro Oda / Shueisha, Toei Animation

Published by Scholastic Inc.

12 11 10 9 8 7 6 5 4 3 2 1   7 8 9 10 11/0

Designed by Phil Falco
Printed in the U.S.A.
First printing, June 2007

PROLOGUE

There once was a man named Gold Roger who was King of the Pirates. He had fame, power, and wealth beyond your wildest dreams.

Before they hung him from the gallows he said: "My fortune is yours for the taking but you'll have to find it first. I've left everything in One Piece." These were his final words.

Ever since, men and women from all over the world set sail for the Grand Line, searching for One Piece, the treasure that would make their dreams come true.

CHAPTER ONE

Captain Kuro's long thin blades glistened in the bright sunlight. Each protruded from a fingertip on his left hand and each one was razor sharp. "My attack has just begun," he said with a chuckle.

Monkey D. Luffy watched with annoyance as the thin man began to sway back and forth. It was the strange motion that Luffy had come to know all too well. During their fight, the thin man had performed this act before sprinting across the battlefield. He would run so fast he seemed invisible. Then, from every direction, he would

1

slash at his opponents with his long blades. This time, however, Luffy was ready for him.

Suddenly, Kuro dashed away into nothingness. Luffy heard his footsteps beating back and forth across the rocky canyon. Luffy also found that if he turned his head just right, he could track the swift pirate from the corner of his eye. Then Luffy did what was impossible for most people; he stretched out both arms until they were each several yards long. He wrapped them around Kuro and dragged him back. Luffy then jumped up and wrapped his thin legs several times around Kuro's waist. To anyone watching, it would seem as if the young boy was made of rubber. Actually, he was. Luffy had eaten the forbidden Gum Gum fruit as a child. Now he truly was a rubber boy.

"Nice dance," Luffy joked as he pulled Kuro closer. He was face-to-face with the villain.

"Get off!" yelled the captain as he struggled to break free. With Luffy's limbs entwined around him, he could no longer wield his bladed glove.

Luffy was ready to finish this battle once and for all. He leaned back and stretched his neck till it was fifty feet long.

"Let go, you headless rubber band!" Kuro ordered.

2

"Gum Gum . . . Bell!" Luffy cried. His head snapped back and slammed into the head of the ensnared pirate. The major head butt knocked Kuro out cold.

"Luffy?" said Nami.

Luffy was pulled from his daydream and found himself back in the booth at the village restaurant. Nami sat across the table and Zolo sat to his left.

"Luffy?" Nami asked again. "What were you thinking about?"

Luffy chuckled and pulled the fish bone from his mouth. "I was thinking about Captain Kuro," he said. "What kind of pirate was he? He had no sense of loyalty."

Captain Kuro had posed as a butler for three years for a wealthy young girl named Kaya. He planned to take over her fortune. Luckily, along with a peculiar young man named Usopp and his ragtag group of Veggie Pirates, Luffy and his crew foiled the evil pirate's plans.

"Here's the deal with pirates," said Nami, "They aren't noble at all."

"She's right," agreed Zolo. "Captain Kuro is more of a typical pirate than you are, Luffy."

3

Luffy couldn't believe it. All of his life, he dreamed of becoming a pirate. He had even met a noble pirate once before — a pirate called Captain Shanks. The pirate had saved Luffy's life and had given him the straw hat from atop his head. Now, Luffy wanted to be more than just a regular pirate. He wanted to become King of the Pirates.

He began his quest by hiding in a wooden barrel and floating out to sea. Soon, he had met Zolo, a feared pirate hunter and master swordsman. Luffy had been fortunate enough to save Zolo's life. Now in his debt, the green-haired swordsman was the first to join Luffy's crew.

Next, they had crossed paths with Nami. The red-haired girl was an expert navigator and accomplished thief. She often stole treasure and treasure maps from the pirates she met. After proving that he wasn't a typical pirate, Luffy convinced her to join his crew.

Unfortunately, Luffy still didn't have a pirate ship to call his own. They had journeyed to this remote island village in a pair of small boats. That's when they had met Usopp. He was best friends with the rich girl, Kaya, and was with Luffy when they first discovered Kuro's evil plans. Together, they had all taken down the wicked pirate captain and his crew.

Zolo pointed to Luffy's empty plate. "If you're done now, could we move on already?"

Luffy sucked the meat off the last fish bone. "I'm ready."

As they were about to leave, Kaya entered the restaurant. "Good, you're here," she said. Her blond hair was pulled back neatly and she wore a fancy summer dress. The young girl seemed all cleaned up after their run-in with the pirates.

"Hi, Miss Kaya," said Luffy.

"I wanted to thank you again for all your help," she said with a smile. "I have a special present for you and I'm sure you'll put it to good use."

A present? thought Luffy. *I wonder what it could be.*

CHAPTER TWO

"It's a real ship!" said Nami.

"You're giving this to us?" asked Luffy. "Unbelievable!"

Luffy and his crew stood on the dock and looked up at a grand ship. It wasn't like the little sailboats in which they had been traveling. This was an honest-to-goodness brand-new ship. Freshly painted white trim accented the polished wooden hull. A thick mast jutted from the center and a smaller one poked up from the rear. Two large sails ruffled in the breeze beneath a crow's nest high atop the mainmast.

Kaya clasped her hands together. "It will make me very happy if you accept."

"Well then, okay!" said Luffy.

One of Kaya's servants, Merry, stood in front of the large vessel. He gestured to the tall ship. "I present to you the S.S. *Merry Go*, named after yours truly, but then of course, I designed her." He began to point to several key pieces of the vessel. "She's a caravel with a solid jib and a central rudder through her stern. In terms of handling, make sure you adjust —"

"You're wasting your time," Nami interrupted with a laugh. She pointed to Luffy and Zolo. "These guys don't get the technical stuff."

Luffy pointed to the front of the ship. "Look at the bow!" A large ram's head jutted from the front of the ship. The carved masthead sat just above a large cannon.

"I posed for that myself," said Merry. He ran a hand across his curly white hair.

"I had it fully stocked because I know you have a long journey ahead of you," Kaya added.

"When you say *stocked*, you're talking food, right?" asked Luffy. Even though he just ate, Luffy couldn't wait to taste all the goodies packed aboard in the ship's galley.

Kay chuckled. "Of course."

"And we'll be rationing yours carefully," said Zolo.

"Help!" cried a voice at the top of the hill.

Everyone turned toward the road leading to the village. A large dark ball bounced into view.

"Oh, no!" said Kaya. "It's Usopp!"

The thin boy was strapped to a large round backpack. The pack was so big that it rolled down the hill with Usopp still attached. He cried for help as he spun around the tumbling pack.

"Strange way to travel, huh, Zolo?" asked Luffy.

"When you're on a roll, you're on a roll," Zolo joked. He moved to the bottom of the hill. "Come on, we better stop him before he slams into the ship."

Luffy stood beside Zolo and they each held out

a foot. Usopp and his pack slammed into their feet with a jarring *THUD!*

"Thanks," said Usopp. "I needed that."

Luffy chuckled. "Any time."

As Luffy and the others boarded their new ship, Kaya stepped over to Usopp. The lanky young man took off his pack and dusted off his overalls.

"Are you sure you want to go out to sea by yourself?" she asked.

Usopp's thin lips spread into a nervous smile. "Yes, Kaya. It's all I ever wanted to do." He took one of her hands. "Please don't try to stop me."

"I won't," said Kaya. She wiped away a tear. "I knew this day would come."

Usopp smiled. "But I'll make you this promise. When I come back I'll have so many great stories! Even better than all the tall tales I've been telling you so far!"

"Good." Kaya giggled. "I look forward to hearing them."

Luffy leaned over the railing and watched their good-byes. Usopp looked up at him and waved. "You guys take care of yourselves," he said. "Maybe our paths will cross some day!"

Luffy cocked his head. "Why would you say that?"

"That's not nice," Usopp said with a frown. "We're all pirates and it's possible that we might meet up with each other on the high seas one day!"

Zolo pulled the swords from his belt and set them on the deck. "Stop your babbling and get on board."

Usopp's eyes widened. "Huh?"

Luffy smiled. "You're part of our crew now," he said. "You helped us defeat Kuro and his men."

Nami put a hand on his shoulder. "You saved the village. You saved me."

With a trembling lip, Usopp simply stared up at Luffy.

"So, are you coming or not?" asked Luffy.

Usopp sprung into the air. "Woopeeee!" He ran behind his large pack and began to roll it toward the gangplank. "I'm a pirate captain after all!"

Luffy laughed. "You're a pirate all right. But I'm the captain. Captain Monkey D. Luffy."

CHAPTER THREE

With Nami's navigational skills, Luffy and his crew set sail for their final destination — the Grand Line. It was a place of myth and legend where the last pirate king, Gold Roger, is said to have hidden his enormous fortune. The treasure was supposed to be so great, it's said that it would make anyone's wildest dreams come true. Gold Roger called it One Piece.

Unfortunately, the Grand Line is fraught with danger. It's said that most who go sailing for it never return. Those who *do* return are so stricken with fear from what they've seen that they're almost like zombies. However, this warning is seldom heeded by the pirates of the seas. The shipping lanes to the Grand Line were full of every kind of pirate imaginable.

Luffy and his crew had a long journey ahead, so they did what they could to pass the time. Usopp painted their very own pirate flag — a skull and cross-bones on a black piece of fabric. Yet, like most pirate flags, this one had a special trait designed just for Luffy's crew. Atop the skull's head sat an orange straw hat, just like Luffy's. Usopp did such a great job, Luffy had him paint the same symbol on the mainsail. Now, anyone who saw them coming would know right away that they were the Straw Hat Pirates.

The small crew sailed for several days on a quiet sea. One afternoon, Zolo climbed to the top deck to take a nap. Just as he was about to close his eyes, the planks below him shook with a thud. He glanced over the railing to see Luffy sliding a large wooden crate across the lower deck.

Nami was stretched out in a nearby deck chair. She pointed to the writing on the crate. "Don't you think you should be careful with something marked *Danger?*"

Luffy pulled off the lid. "I just found this belowdeck!"

Usopp and Nami joined Luffy beside the open crate. From the upper deck, Zolo could see past them and into the box below. Several large black balls were stored inside.

"Cannon shells?" asked Nami.

"Yeah," Luffy replied. "We have a cannon, so why not learn how to use it?"

Usopp jutted a thumb at his chest. "Well then, leave it to me!" he said. "I have plenty of experience with cannons. In fact, I hitched a ride on a cannon-ball halfway across the world when I was . . ."

No one was listening to Usopp's tall tale. Nami went back to her deck chair while Luffy was examining the cannon at the front of the ship.

Luffy rubbed his chin. "Now, how does this thing work?" He turned toward the upper deck. "Zolo, do you know how to work this thing?"

Zolo quickly laid back and closed his eyes. He was a swordsman, not a gunner. Besides, he didn't feel like lugging cannon shells at the moment.

"Zolo's catching some Z's," said Nami.

Luffy sighed. "What a bore."

Nami unrolled the wrinkled map showing the way to the Grand Line. "If we go a little farther south, there's a rock that would make for great target practice!"

"Let's go!" said Usopp.

Zolo yawned as he heard the others scramble to change course. Usopp was even beginning another tall tale. "I think I saw that very rock on my trip around the world! Hey! Is anyone listening?"

Usopp's voice faded as Zolo drifted off to sleep. Soon, he dreamt he was a little boy again, back in his old village.

CHAPTER FOUR

When Zolo was younger, he was a rambunctious child, full of anger and competitiveness. He was always looking for trouble. He was always looking for a fight.

It was a beautiful summer day as he strolled through his small village. He passed several cottages and shops, all full of the quiet townsfolk who were his neighbors. However, Zolo's attention was drawn to sounds of battle. He marched down the main street and stopped at the local dojo — a martial arts school. Zolo stepped through the open doorway and saw several students fighting with bamboo practice swords. Each wore a green gi — a two-piece uniform worn by martial arts fighters. The cracks of their bamboo swords echoed through the large open room as they fought. The soft mat covering the floor trembled as a few students were struck and fell to the ground.

Zolo watched for a moment as they ran through their drills. They didn't seem so tough. Certainly they weren't as tough as the mighty Zolo. After all, even at his young age, Zolo had bested every fighter he had come across.

"Hey!" Zolo shouted. "Who wants some?"

The students froze and stared at him. No one said a word. Zolo thought they must have been very frightened.

"I said who wants some?" he asked again. "Your best student! I'll fight him!"

The sensei — their instructor — was a thin man with glasses and long black hair pulled back in a ponytail. He stepped over to Zolo. "You do know this is a dojo and not a day care," he said smugly.

Zolo crossed his arms. "You do know that in the next village over, not a single person could beat me."

The martial arts master smiled. "Very well, challenge accepted." He waved Zolo inside. "But if you lose, you must become my student."

Zolo nodded in agreement. He had no intention of being one of this guy's students. But, then again, he had no intention of losing either. He scanned the faces of the students. All of the boys were slightly older than he, but he didn't care. He knew he could beat any of them easily.

The master turned and shouted. "Kuina!"

A young girl with short black hair ran in from another room. "I'm here, Sensei." She too held a wooden practice sword.

"What's this?" asked Zolo. "There's no way she can be your best student!"

The sensei smiled. "Kuina may be a girl, but she's more skillful than even my oldest pupils. And that's not just because she's my daughter."

Zolo was furious. Surely this instructor was toying with him. He must think Zolo was so weak that he couldn't even beat a girl. Nevertheless, if this man wanted to play games with him, fine. He'd beat his daughter for sure.

That'll teach him. Zolo's hands formed into tight fists. "Let's go!"

The master gave a small bow and walked across the practice floor. "Follow me, young one."

The rest of the students took seats against the far wall. Only Kuina stood in the center of the room.

Zolo followed the martial arts master to a wooden barrel full of practice swords. He gestured toward them.

"I can use any of these?" asked Zolo.

"Take your pick," replied the master.

Zolo wasn't taking any chances. He grabbed as many swords as he could hold. He held four in each hand and three in his mouth. After all, the more swords the better. If he had so many and the girl only had one, he was sure to win.

The master let slip a small chuckle. "Are you ready, young one?"

"I . . . sure . . . am!" Zolo said through clenched teeth. It was difficult to speak with all those swords in his mouth.

The master lead Zolo to the center of the room to stand beside the girl. "Bow to the dojo!" he instructed.

Both Zolo and Kuina gave a quick bow to the

small shrine on the dojo's main wall. One of the swords slipped from Zolo's mouth.

"And now bow to your opponent," the master continued.

Zolo and Kuina turned and bowed to each other. Another sword dropped from his mouth, leaving only one. Zolo wasn't worried, though. His hands still held more than enough to beat the young girl.

The master stepped back as the two faced off. "Begin!"

Immediately, the girl struck with amazing speed. It was all Zolo could do to bring up both hands and keep her sword from bopping him on the head. Her attack was so strong that she knocked him flat on his back. All his swords went flying.

"Lucky," Zolo growled as he quickly got to his feet. He reached down and grabbed a sword in each hand. Stepping closer, he held one sword out and the other over his head.

Kuina raised an eyebrow. "So, you have studied the way of two swords?"

"Heck, no," Zolo replied. "This is my first time even holding one!"

"Your first time?" asked the master.

Come on, I'm stronger than this! *Zolo told himself.* I can't let myself lose to some girl!

With swords flailing, he charged toward Kuina. She effortlessly sidestepped his attack. Then, from out of nowhere, her sword slammed down on the top of his head. Zolo dropped his two swords and fell to the mat.

"Match over," said the master. "Kuina wins!"

Kuina stepped closer. "He fights like a wild boar!"

"Be nice now," said the master.

She slammed the blunt tip of her practice sword beside Zolo's face. "By the way," she said, "you might want to master one sword before you use two." Zolo put a hand on her sword and pulled himself to his feet. She shook the wooden blade from his hand and walked across the room. "Oh, well. You're my father's problem now anyway."

"A deal's a deal," said the master.

Zolo felt his face turn red as he boiled with anger. "Yes, it is," *he growled.* "And I'll practice and practice and practice!" *He pointed at Kuina.* "You'll see! I'll defeat you! Just you wait!"

Kuina laughed. "That will never happen."

CHAPTER FIVE

For the next year, Zolo did as he promised. Wearing his own green gi, he took lessons from the master and practiced every chance he could. He performed countless drills with his bamboo sword against the large wooden practice posts. He dangled a large rock from a rope in his teeth for strength training. When the entire class ran laps in a nearby field, Zolo carried a student on his back and still outran them all.

Zolo was also a quick study. He became quite skilled first with one sword and then with two. However, his training was more than mere swordsmanship. His new sensei taught him all about self-discipline and honor. Zolo no longer roamed the countryside picking fights and causing trouble. He concentrated not just on fighting — but fighting honorably. Now his goal was to become the most powerful swordsman in the world.

Zolo was well on his way to his goal. He slowly surpassed the skills of other students his age. In training combat, he defeated the older and more experienced students. He even defeated a few grown men who dropped by for practice. However, there was still one student he couldn't defeat — Kuina. In countless sparring sessions, the older girl continued to put him to the mat. No matter how skillfully he used both practice swords, she could always defeat him with one.

"It's not the swords," she kept reminding him. "It's the swordsman . . . or the swordswoman."

One night, Zolo snuck into the dojo to retrieve some real swords. He found two long katanas with black rope handles. The sharp samurai swords rattled in their wooden scabbards as he ran to find Kuina. He spotted her walking down a deserted lane.

"Zolo?" she asked with surprise.

"Finally, I found you," he said.

"What do you want, Zolo?" asked Kuina.

"I want to challenge you to a sword fight!" growled Zolo. His hands tightened on the swords. "To decide which one of us is really the best, once and for all." He held out the swords. "And we decide with these!"

Kuina narrowed her eyes. "You're on."

Zolo waited in a nearby field as the girl ran back to get her sword. A cool breeze blew through his green hair but it did nothing to cool his obsession. When Kuina returned, she carried a beautiful katana with a woven white grip. The two opponents unsheathed their weapons and faced off. Three razor-sharp blades glistened in the moonlight.

Zolo attacked at once, his two swords a blur as he swiped and chopped at Kuina. But as always, the young girl parried each blow with ease. Zolo wasn't discouraged; he continued to strike with every attack he knew. Kuina did the same, and soon, the rapid sound of clanking metal filled the night air.

Zolo stepped back to catch his breath. He shook the sweat from his eyes and panted through gritted teeth.

"Real swords are much heavier, aren't they?" asked Kuina. She wasn't breathing hard at all. And only a few beads of sweat dotted her forehead. "What?" she asked. "Too tired to talk?"

Her coolness infuriated him. He had hoped that challenging her with real swords would shake her confidence. Yet she was as skillful as always. It seemed that no matter how hard he trained, she still had the upper hand.

As if reading his mind, the young girl suddenly charged him. Zolo raised his blades in defense but it was too late. With one skillful swipe, she knocked both swords from his hands and knocked him backward. The blades tumbled through the night as Zolo tumbled backward.

When he slid to a stop on the ground, Kuina stabbed the dirt with her sword. The sharp blade dug in, mere inches from his face. "Well, guess we know who's best," she said.

Zolo's eyes filled with tears. "What's wrong with me?" He struck the dirt with his fists. "I just can't beat you. I'm not strong enough!"

Kuina pulled the sword from the ground and wiped the blade clean. "Not yet you're not. But you will be."

Zolo sat up and wiped his eyes.

"You're a boy," Kuina said. "As you grow older, you'll become stronger. And the stronger you get, the better swordsman you'll be." Kuina sheathed her sword and hung her head. "It's just a matter of time."

"What are you talking about?" Zolo asked as he got to his feet.

"My father told me himself," she explained. "Boys are stronger than girls." A lone tear streamed down her cheek. "So a girl can never be the best. That's just the way it all works out."

Zolo's lip trembled. "Don't tell me this stuff!" he yelled. "You're my very best opponent!"

"Look, Zolo . . ."

"It doesn't matter that you're a girl!" he shouted. "Being the best swordsman is about heart! And you have tons of heart! And don't let your dad or anyone else tell you otherwise! You got that?"

Kuina stared down at him with unbelieving eyes. Zolo marched closer. "Promise me! One day either you or

I will become the best swordsman in all the land! I want to hear you say it!"

Kuina stared at him for a long time. Finally, she smiled. "Yes. One day. One of us will be the best."

Zolo reached out an open hand. Kuina shook it. "I promise!" they said together.

CHAPTER SIX

For the next several months, both Zolo and Kuina trained harder than ever. Zolo continued to increase his skill with two swords while Kuina surpassed her father's expectations. It turned out that Zolo had been right. It didn't matter that she was a girl. She began sparring with trained men from other villages. She defeated everyone who faced her, no matter how old they were. Her reputation grew as accomplished fighters from all over the land came to test their skills against her.

Zolo knew she was ahead of him in years and in practice. Therefore, he trained harder than anyone could *imagine. He beat his bamboo swords against rope-wrapped practice poles until both were nothing more than splinters. He increased the size of rock weights until he was able to hold small boulders suspended from a rope in his mouth. He tossed ropes over tree limbs and attached the ends to more stones so he could lift one with each hand. And all the while, he kept the large weight between his teeth. He made his jaws strong so he could hold a third sword between his teeth someday. He would wield as many swords as necessary to be the best. Soon he'd be good enough to beat Kuina in honorable combat.*

One day, as Zolo was training with the heavy stones, he saw two other students standing at the edge of the forest. They didn't say a word. They just stood there watching him. One of them was crying.

"What's the matter?" asked Zolo through clenched teeth.

"Kuina's at the hospital," one of the boys replied. "She was fighting some man and defeated him."

"But then he came back with friends," added the other student. "They hurt her bad. All because this man was embarrassed to be beaten by a girl."

Zolo let go of the ropes, and the rocks slammed into

the ground. He tore past the boys and ran to the hospital. Tears streamed from his eyes all the way.

When he arrived, the nurses wouldn't let him see her. Instead, he was met by Kuina's father.

"Why?!" asked Zolo.

"Follow me," said his sensei.

He took Zolo back to the dojo. There they knelt before the tiny shrine on the main wall. Kuina's father reached over and opened a long wooden box. He pulled out Kuina's sword, her real swords, and placed them under the altar.

"Life can be cruel, Zolo," said the master. "Kuina wanted nothing more on this Earth than to be the best. She practiced hard ever since she was a child and was well on her way to meeting that goal. Then you arrived."

Zolo didn't answer. He tried to fight back the steady stream of tears instead.

"She bested you many times," his master continued. "But I thought because she was a girl, you would eventually overpower her. However, she never gave up." He unsheathed the sword and examined the blade. It glistened in the afternoon light. "Kuina taught me, her sensei and father, that it's not whether you're a boy or a girl, it's about your heart." He sheathed the sword and stood. "It was her dream to be the best, Zolo. Perhaps you knew that more than anyone else." He placed the sword onto the small shrine on the wall. "But now, because of her injury, she'll never be able to fight again."

Zolo couldn't believe that he would never be able to spar against Kuina again. At first, she had been his sworn enemy. But as time went on, they had become fast friends. They had pushed each other to be the very best. Yet they both knew that someday they would have to fight each other one last time. That battle would decide who was best, once and for all. Now, that day would never come. Zolo would never know if he could have ever been good enough to beat her.

But Zolo wasn't heartbroken. He was no longer the arrogant brat who first challenged the entire dojo. Now his thoughts were only of Kuina. He couldn't bear the thought of Kuina's dreams going unfulfilled. His master was right; he knew how Kuina felt better than anyone. They shared the same dream.

Zolo wiped his eyes and bowed his head. "Sensei, that sword," he whispered. "Please give it to me."

"Kuina's sword?" asked the master.

"We made a promise," said Zolo. "That one of us would become the best. And if it can't be her, then I'll do it for *her*!" He got to his feet and looked his master in the eye. "I'll train harder than I did before. And I'll never forget the heart that Kuina fought with. Never."

Kuina's father smiled. He removed the sword from the shrine and offered it to Zolo. "I entrust you with Kuina's sword," he said. "And her dreams."

Zolo took the sword and bowed to his master. "You won't be sorry."

CHAPTER SEVEN

For seven more years, Zolo trained longer and harder than any of the other students. He had worked hard so his muscles were tight and his balance was steady. His bamboo practice swords had long been abandoned. The real samurai swords no longer felt heavy in his hands. Like a true swordsman, the swords were now an extension of his body. He held one of his black swords in each hand and Kuina's white sword in his mouth. His unique fighting style soon bested all the other students — and even his master.

As a final test, Zolo faced off against a giant boulder dangling from a thick tree branch. He unsheathed all three swords and crouched. Then, with lightning speed, he attacked. In the blink of an eye, Zolo found himself on the other side of the dangling boulder. He glanced over his shoulder as the rock slowly fell apart in three clean pieces.

His master clapped as Zolo quickly sheathed his swords. Zolo then turned and bowed to his sensei.

"That was the final test," said his master. "You've become faster than the human eye. There's no more I can teach you."

The next day, Zolo prepared to leave. He tucked the three swords into his green waistband and packed his belongings. His sensei met him at the edge of the village.

"In these past eight years you've learned so much," said the master.

"Yes," Zolo said with a respectful bow. "And now I must leave and become the best."

His master returned the bow. "Yes, my student," he replied. "Become the very best. Do it for Kuina."

Zolo left that day and never returned. He also

never gave up on his vow to become the very best swords-
man in the land.

BOOM!

Zolo was ripped from his dream by the sound of cannon fire.

CHAPTER EIGHT

Luffy watched as the cannonball flew toward the dark mass on the horizon. Just as Nami had predicted, the towering rock was perfect for their target practice. Unfortunately, a plume of water shot into the air where the cannonball splashed down — nowhere near the rock.

"It missed by a mile," said Luffy.

"What are you two doing down there?" barked Zolo. He frowned as he leaned over from the upper deck. They had woken him from his nap.

"Practicing with the cannon," Luffy replied.

He looked down the barrel of the large gun at the rock in the distance. "But I can't get off a straight shot."

"Hey, not a problem," said Usopp. "I can fix that easy!" Luffy loaded another shell as Usopp shoved the cannon a few inches to the left. "Judging by that last trajectory, this should be about right." Usopp checked his aim again, then pulled the cord. "Fire!"

BOOM!

Another cannonball sailed toward the rock. This time, its aim was true. It smashed into the towering stone, shattering it to pieces.

"Unbelievable!" yelled Luffy. "And on your first shot!"

Usopp's eyes widened. "It really hit?" he asked. Then he looked back at Luffy. "I mean, of course it hit. I told you I know how to work this thing!"

"Yeah, you sure do!" Luffy agreed. "Which is why you're going to be the ship's gunner!"

"Wait, then who will be captain?" asked Usopp.

Luffy shook his head. "I've *been* the captain, crazy."

After the successful target practice, everyone went into the ship's galley — the kitchen — for a snack. The small room had a large pantry, a small sink, and an old iron stove. Luffy and his crew sat on benches on either side of the long wooden table. They happily ate some apples. The ship had been fully stocked when they set sail, but supplies were already dwindling. It wouldn't be long before they had to stop somewhere for more provisions.

"Okay, Luffy, I've decided that I'll be the ship's gunner!" Usopp announced. "But if you can't handle the captain thing, we'll switch back."

Luffy chuckled. "You got it!" He glanced around the galley. "But you know, before we make our way to the Grand Line, we still have one more crew position to fill."

"You're right," agreed Nami. "The ship's galley is not much use without one. Good call, Luffy!"

"Yeah, smart thinking," added Zolo.

Luffy smiled. "Thanks, you guys. A singer *is* pretty essential!"

"A singer?!" asked Usopp.

"I thought you meant a cook!" said Nami.

Zolo laughed and shook his head. "No, that would have been a *good* idea."

Luffy burst into laughter. "Someone has to sing all those cool pirate songs!"

"Show yourselves!" boomed a voice from outside.

Luffy glanced around the galley. His entire crew was inside. Who else could be on the ship? He threw open the door and looked down to the main deck. A dark-haired man with a tattoo on the side of his face glared back at him. The man held a long jagged sword.

Luffy stepped up to the railing. "Well, here I am. Who are you?"

"You be quiet!" roared the man. He raised his sword. "*I'm* asking the questions!"

Luffy barely got out of the way as the sword sliced through the wooden railing. Then he jumped back again as the man chopped away another section. Luffy leaped onto the main deck and backed away from the crazed swordsman.

"I'll take out you and all your pirate friends, you

scoundrel!" The man swung madly at Luffy. "I won't let a band of cutthroats like you hurt my comrade!"

"What are you talking about?" asked Luffy.

The man answered by charging for another attack. Luffy quickly circled around the mainmast. The man tried to come after him, but Luffy kept the large post between them. The swordsman was so crazed, he raised the sword as if he were going to chop down the mast itself.

"Stop destroying my ship!" yelled Luffy. He stretched out both arms and grabbed the swordsman's head. Letting his rubber limbs snap back, he slammed the man's head into the mast.

The man dropped his sword and fell to the deck. "That was a lucky shot," he groaned.

"What's your problem?" asked Luffy.

Zolo poked his head out of the galley. "Johnny? Is that you?"

The man's head jerked upward. "Huh? Who dares call me by my . . ." He pulled down his thin sunglasses. "Zolo?"

Zolo smiled. "I thought I recognized that voice."

CHAPTER NINE

Zolo couldn't believe his eyes. It was one of his former pirate-hunting partners. Before he teamed up with Luffy, Zolo had worked with another pair of fighters — Johnny and Yosaku. He hadn't seen either of them in a very long time.

Johnny leaped to his feet. "What in the world are you doing on a pirate ship?"

Zolo gave a nervous chuckle. "It's a long story," he replied. "Say, where's Yosaku?"

Johnny pointed to the side of the ship. "He's over here. Come quick!"

Zolo jumped over the railing and ran across the deck after Johnny. When they reached the side, his former comrade pointed to a small boat floating beside the *Merry Go*. Yosaku was sprawled across the deck of the smaller vessel. The thin man looked almost as Zolo remembered. He even wore the same dingy green trench coat and orange headband. Unfortunately, what didn't look the same was his health. His old friend was extremely pale, panting, and unconscious.

"He's in bad shape," said Johnny.

Zolo and Johnny jumped into the smaller boat and hoisted Yosaku aboard the *Merry Go*. They gently spread him across a mat on the main deck. Luffy and Usopp came closer but didn't say a word.

"What's wrong with him?" asked Zolo.

Johnny shook his head. "I don't know. He was fit as a fiddle just a few days ago. Then he went pale and became bedridden." He sat back and stared at his sick friend. "It was awful. His teeth started to fall out, old wounds started to open, and his breathing started to sound like a rubber squeeze toy! I didn't know what to do!"

Zolo touched Yosaku's forehead. It was cold and wet with sweat.

"So, to think I anchored my ship next to this great big rock," said Johnny. He glared up at Luffy and Usopp. "And that's when one of you shot a cannonball at me!"

Usopp pointed to Luffy. "It was him!"

"No, him!" Luffy pointed back.

Johnny buried his face in his hands. "When your cannonball hit, we barely got away with our lives!" He put a hand on Yosaku's chest. The man's breathing quickened. "But it's no use," said Johnny. "My buddy's a goner."

"Don't be silly," said Nami. She strolled down the steps and knelt beside the sick man.

"Nami?" asked Zolo.

She opened one of Yosaku's eyelids and examined his glazed eye. Then she opened his mouth and pulled out his tongue. She turned it over, checking both sides.

"Stop that!" Johnny grabbed her wrist with a trembling hand. "Have a little respect for my friend! He hasn't passed yet!"

Nami put a hand on Johnny's face and pushed him away. She turned to the others. "Luffy, Usopp! There are limes in the galley, go get them!"

Luffy and Usopp scrambled over each other as they ran up the steps and into the galley. They quickly returned with a barrel full of limes.

"Cut up those limes and drip the juice into his mouth," she instructed.

Luffy and Usopp did as she said. One by one, they dripped the sour juice into the sick man's throat. Even unconscious, he lapped up every drop.

Nami stood and joined Zolo and Johnny. "He has scurvy," she said.

"Scurvy?" asked Johnny.

"Yeah, it's a disease," she explained. "But he should be okay now."

Johnny hugged her. "What a lifesaver! Thank you! Thank you!" he shouted. "You're such a doll!"

Nami's eyes widened as she pushed him away. "Let's not ever call me that again, okay?" She turned to Luffy and Usopp. "A generation ago, scurvy was a sailor's worst enemy. If someone didn't get enough vitamin C, their body started to fail them, like your friend here."

"You sure know a lot, Nami," said Luffy. He squeezed another lime over the man's mouth.

"Yeah," agreed Usopp. "How fascinating!"

Nami growled and Zolo stepped back. He knew what was coming.

"You guys!" she yelled. "As pirates, you should know this stuff! Or you'll end up just like him!"

Suddenly, Yosaku sputtered. He spit out a lime peel and got to his feet. His color was back and his eyes were once again full of life. Johnny ran to him and gave him a big hug.

"We're cured! We're cured! We're cured!" the two chanted as they bounced up and down. "Three cheers for limes!" yelled Johnny. "Hip-hip-hooray! Hip-hip-hooray! Hip-hip-hooray!"

"Okay, you're both nuts!" yelled Nami. "Who are you guys? First you're disease-ridden and now you're dancing?"

"That's Johnny and Yosaku," said Zolo. "They used to be my pirate-hunting partners."

Johnny grinned. "Those were the days, eh, Zolo?"

"We sure had a lot of fun," said Yosaku.

Zolo laughed. "Yeah, who would have thought we'd run into each other out here!"

"I know," said Johnny. His grin disappeared. "A pirate hunter on a pirate ship?"

"Yeah, what's the deal, Zolo?" asked Yosaku.

"Aw, these pirates are okay," said Zolo. He patted Yosaku on the back. "After all, they cured you, didn't they?"

With Zolo's touch, Yosaku crumpled to the deck, unconscious again.

"Oh, no! Yosaku!" said Johnny. "What's wrong with him now?"

"He'll be all right," said Nami. "He just should have dozed instead of danced after that scurvy scare."

Zolo and Johnny picked up Yosaku and laid him out on Nami's deck chair. He snored peacefully.

"Well, I'm going to get scurvy unless I get some good food on this ship pretty soon!" said Usopp.

"No, you're not!" barked Nami. "That soufflé surprise I made this morning was very healthy."

Usopp grimaced. "Yeah, it tasted healthy, all right."

She poked Usopp in the chest. "Well, you try coming up with a recipe for turnips, bread, and limes."

"Too bad there isn't someone who can cook for us," said Luffy. "Wait! There could be, if we got a chef!"

"That's what I said before," said Nami.

"Good idea, Luffy," agreed Usopp. "Every good pirate ship needs a good chef!"

Nami shook her head with disgust. Zolo tried to keep from laughing.

Johnny rubbed his chin. "Say, I know where to find a good chef. But I can't be sure he'll join us."

"Super!" said Luffy. "Where to? Let's go!"

"It's near the Grand Line," he explained. "But some rough customers frequent that place." Johnny glanced up at the sun, then pointed off the port bow. "It's that way! North by Northeast!"

CHAPTER TEN

They followed Johnny's directions until a large ship appeared on the horizon. As they sailed closer, Luffy saw that the ship was in the shape of a giant fish. A fish head with a gaping mouth was attached to its bow, and a giant tail acted as its rudder.

"There it is!" announced Johnny. "The bistro of the brine, Baratie!"

"Baratie?" asked Nami.

"It's a famous restaurant," Johnny explained. "All the seafarers go there."

"I think I've heard of this place," remarked Zolo.

As the floating restaurant grew closer, they saw several smaller ships docked to the side of the restaurant. Through the windows, they saw many patrons sitting at fancy dinner tables. Before long, the delicious aroma of freshly cooked food filled the air.

Johnny took a deep breath. "Nice, don't you agree?"

Luffy's mouth was already watering. "I hope the food tastes as good as it smells," he replied. He couldn't wait to sample some of their dishes. "Yum!"

Yosaku staggered to his feet. His attention wasn't on the restaurant in front of them. He pointed to the right. "Uh, what is that navy ship doing here?"

Everyone was so enthralled with Baratie that they didn't notice the large white ship sailing alongside them. The vessel was slightly larger than the *Merry Go* and its decks were full of busy crewmen.

Usopp pointed to one of its large cannons. "Hey! They're not going to fire on us, are they?"

Zolo crossed his arms. "Well, if they do, they'll have to contend with me!"

A tall man in a white suit stepped onto the navy

ship's main deck. He had short pink hair, a scar on his right cheek, and a metal plate on his right fist. He gazed up at the top of the *Merry Go*. "I haven't seen that pirate flag before."

Johnny and Yosaku dashed toward the cabin door. "Actually, Mr. Navy Man, we're not pirates!" said Johnny.

"Yeah," agreed Yosaku as he followed Johnny into the cabin.

The tall man laughed. "Sure, and I'm not Lieutenant 'Ironfist' Fullbody, commander of the sea!" He scanned the rest of Luffy's crew. "Who's the captain over there? Identify yourself!"

Luffy stepped forward. "It's me! Monkey D. Luffy!"

Usopp joined him. "Yeah, and me! Usopp the great!"

Luffy rolled his eyes. "And we just made our pirate flag yesterday!"

"And yesterday, I made that flag!" said Usopp.

Luffy jabbed Usopp with his elbow.

Lieutenant Fullbody laughed. "How cute.

49

You're beginners." He pointed to the cabin where Johnny and Yosaku poked their heads out of the doorway. "However, I've seen those two before. You're those two-bit bounty hunters . . . Yosaku and Johnny."

Johnny stormed onto the deck. "What did you say?"

"And it looks as if you finally got caught by a band of pirates," Fullbody added.

"You got it all wrong," barked Johnny.

The lieutenant laughed. "Oh, *sure* I do."

Just then, a blond woman stepped out of the navy ship's cabin. She put an arm around Lieutenant Fullbody. "Let's go, sweetie. I'm hungry."

"Sure," said the lieutenant. He turned to two of his naval crewmen. "As for our pirate friends, take care of them."

The crewmen saluted. "Yes, sir!" They scrambled to one of the cannons, loaded it, and aimed it at the *Merry Go*.

"Uh, bad news, guys!" said Usopp. "They're about to fire at us!"

"Leave that to me!" said Luffy. He jumped onto the railing and wrapped his legs around the wooden slats. Then he stretched out one arm and grabbed the mainmast. He stretched the other and latched onto the ship's masthead.

Ka-VOOM!

The cannon blasted a shell right at them. Luffy positioned his body to catch it, and the speeding ball slammed into his stomach. He held tight with his arms and legs as his entire body absorbed the blow. With his arms and legs stretching, he flew out over the water like a giant rubber band.

"Gum Gum Slingshot!" shouted Luffy. He intended to shoot the cannonball back to the navy ship. Unfortunately, his left hand slipped off the masthead. Luffy's body swung around to the back of the *Merry Go*. Instead of aiming at the enemy, his body now faced Baratie. When he snapped back, the cannonball flew through the air and slammed into the small cabin at the top of the restaurant.

CRASH!

"Uh-oh." Luffy cringed as planks and shingles

exploded from the roof of the cabin. Smoke billowed from the new hole in the roof.

In a small dinghy, Fullbody's men rowed the lieutenant and his dinner date toward the restaurant. He looked up at the restaurant and laughed. "I guess smoked salmon's on the menu now."

CHAPTER ELEVEN

After they docked the ship, Luffy scrambled aboard the restaurant to see if anyone was hurt. He was immediately apprehended by two men in white smocks and white chef hats. They hauled him up to the small smoking cabin.

"Chef Zeff," said one of the men. "We caught the jerk that caused the explosion!"

They dragged Luffy inside and slammed him to the floor. A thick haze filled the small captain's quarters. Smoking debris covered the bed, trunks, and dresser. Towering over Luffy was an enormous man wearing a super-tall chef's hat. His long blond mustache was braided on each side. The braids kept his mustache pointed straight out on either side of his face. He peered down at Luffy with angry eyes.

Luffy bowed humbly. "I'm sorry! I'm sorry!"

"You'll be sorry!" growled Chef Zeff.

Luffy crawled closer and noticed that the man was missing a leg. All that propped him up was a wooden peg. "And I'm so sorry for blowing up your leg!" Luffy added.

"Nah! That wasn't you, kid!" The chef swung his peg leg, kicking Luffy in the gut. "But you did bruise me up a bit."

"What are you going to do to me?" asked Luffy. He got to his feet and rubbed his stomach. "I'll gladly pay for the damages."

"Oh?" said Zeff.

Luffy turned out his pockets. "Only, I have no money."

Chef Zeff sat back on his bed. He propped his peg leg up on a trunk. "Well, if you have no money, then how do you plan to pay for the damages?"

"Uh, I'll make good somehow," Luffy replied.

"Yes, you will," Zeff said as he smiled. "Working here free for a year!"

"Sure, sounds good," said Luffy. "It's a deal!"

"Good!" said Zeff.

Luffy was quite relieved. For a moment there, he thought that . . . Wait a minute! *Did he say a year?* "A whole year?" Luffy asked.

The chef laughed. "That's right. One year."

Luffy held up a finger. "Actually, how about just one week."

"One week?" Zeff roared. "Are you joking?"

Luffy held up two fingers. "Two weeks, then."

Chef Zeff leaned forward and tapped Luffy's head with the end of his long hat. "Do you really think you can destroy someone's restaurant, injure the head chef, and get off with a measly two weeks of work?"

"All right," Luffy added a finger. "Three weeks."

"You're dreaming, kid!" Zeff sprung off the bed and slammed his peg leg into Luffy. The rubber boy flew across the room and bounced off a wall.

Luffy got to his feet and dusted off his vest.

"Listen, it took me ten years to become a pirate. And now that I've become one, well, I can't just give up a year of my life."

"I completely understand your point," said Zeff. He strolled over to Luffy. "So let's come up with a quicker way to solve this." The chef grabbed a saw from a nearby table. He reached out his peg leg and poked one of Luffy's ankles. "That leg there! Leave it with me!"

"You're crazy!" said Luffy.

Zeff laughed. "Crazy for that leg of yours!"

CHAPTER TWELVE

Zolo led the way as he, Usopp, and Nami entered the restaurant. Johnny and Yosaku had decided to stay aboard the *Merry Go*. They didn't want to run into Lieutenant Fullbody again. Zolo wasn't frightened, though. He had fought against the navy captain Axe-Hand Morgan. Morgan was a giant of a man with an axe at the end of one arm. Some skinny naval lieutenant with a puny metal plate on his fist just didn't spook him.

The inside of Baratie was just as impressive as the outside. It seemed that the entire main deck of the ship had been converted to a fancy dining hall. Several round tables were scattered about the large room. Each one was covered with fine white table linen and shiny dinnerware. In the center of the room, a spiral staircase snaked around the mainmast. Based on the sounds emanating from the room above, the staircase must have led to the kitchen.

As Zolo and the others sat down, they spotted Fullbody right away. The lieutenant sat at a smaller table nearby. The blond woman from the ship sat across from him. It seemed that he and his date were the center of attention. Everyone in the restaurant was talking about them.

"Hey, look!" said one of the customers. "There's Lieutenant Fullbody sitting over there! In the flesh!"

"The naval officer?" asked another.

"Wow," said a woman. "He sure is cute."

The lieutenant glanced around the room. He seemed to be eating up all the attention.

"Everyone in this room is looking at you," said his dinner date.

Fullbody took her hand and kissed it. "Only because I'm with a lady like you."

Zolo rolled his eyes.

Just then, a slim man in a black suit strolled toward Fullbody and his date. The man had blond hair, and a lollipop stick poked out of his mouth. He carried a tray with two bowls of soup and a bottle of juice wrapped in cloth. He handed out the soup and poured the juice into their glasses.

Fullbody sipped the juice and swished it around his mouth. "Superb grape juice!" He spoke loudly so everyone in the restaurant could hear. The man in the black suit was about to unwrap the bottle when Fullbody stopped him. "Wait, let me guess," said the lieutenant. He held the glass up and studied the dark juice. "It's a fifty-four . . . with a delicate bouquet, full bodied, and very dry. From the north of Mikkyuo, at the Buruga Vineyard!" He took another sip. "Yes, there's no doubt about it."

Zolo glanced around the restaurant. Everyone seemed to be quite impressed with Fullbody's vast knowledge. The lieutenant's date seemed doubly impressed.

Fullbody leaned back in his chair. "Am I right, waiter?"

The man unwrapped the bottle, revealing the label. "Sorry, but you're not, sir." He casually grabbed the lieutenant's wrist and slapped a spoon into his hand. "Now then, soup's on." He turned and walked back toward the staircase. "Enjoy it while it's hot."

Nami snickered. "And he was so sure of himself," she whispered.

Everyone else in the restaurant chuckled quietly at the arrogant display.

Before climbing the stairs, the man in the black suit stopped and looked back at Fullbody. "Oh, and my name is Sanji. I wouldn't want you to guess that wrong, too."

Many of the patrons couldn't hold back their laughter. The lieutenant snarled as he peered around the room.

The woman at Fullbody's table held up her glass. "It's still good."

Fullbody glared at her. "What?"

"The juice," she replied.

The lieutenant picked up his glass and downed the last sip. "Oh yes. It's quite good," he grumbled. "A very fine vineyard, wherever it is."

Amused, Zolo watched as the navy lieutenant sat and fumed with anger. His date began eating her soup, but the man didn't touch a drop. The lieutenant glanced down and saw an insect crawl across the floor. He quickly stamped on it with his boot. At first, Zolo thought the lieutenant was merely taking out his frustrations on the unlucky bug. But to his amazement, Fullbody leaned down and picked up the twitching insect. He dropped it into his soup and smiled. Zolo wondered what he was up to.

"Waiter! Look!" yelled Fullbody. He had everyone's attention.

Sanji turned around, strolled down the stairs, and approached their table. "I'm as much of a waiter as you are a juice connoisseur," he said. "I'm the assistant chef." Sanji then turned to the lady and took her hand. "And you, my lady, are beautiful." She giggled as he lightly kissed her hand. "Which makes me wonder what you're doing with a tasteless buffoon such as this!"

Fullbody slammed his fist on the table. "Tasteless is serving soup with a fly in it, my dear sir!"

He pointed his spoon at the bowl in front of him. "What is this?"

"What's what?" asked Sanji.

The lieutenant growled. "What is this fly doing in my soup?"

"Well, I'm not positive." Sanji leaned over and examined the dish. "But I think it's the backstroke."

Zolo snickered along with everyone else in the restaurant.

Sanji turned and winked at his audience. "Of course, the butterfly would be a more fitting style, don't you think?"

The restaurant erupted with laughter. Even Fullbody's date giggled at the witty remark.

"You fool!" Fullbody roared. He stood and raised his hand high above his head. "You have no clue with whom you're toying!" He slammed his iron-clad fist on the table, breaking it in two. Dishes, silverware, and soup flew everywhere.

A hush fell over the restaurant. Zolo put a hand on his swords. He didn't know if this Sanji needed help or not. But if he did, Zolo would be more than happy to take on the rude navy lieutenant.

To Zolo's surprise, Sanji knelt before Lieutenant Fullbody. At first, it appeared as if he was asking for forgiveness. But then he ran his fingers through the puddle of spilled soup.

"Good food should never be wasted," said Sanji. He glared up at Fullbody. "Nor should a perfectly good opportunity to teach a rude pig some manners."

"How dare you! I'm a customer!" Fullbody boomed. "You're just a lowly chef!" He stepped forward and slammed his foot onto Sanji's hand. "Stay in your place, cook! Right at my feet!" He ground his hand beneath his heal. "Understand?!"

"Stop it!" yelled Fullbody's date. She stood and grabbed the lieutenant's arm. "Let him go!" Fullbody sneered as he shoved her away. She tumbled to the floor. "What is wrong with you, you brute?"

Sanji glared up at the lieutenant. "You get your own way a lot, don't you, mister?"

"So what?" asked Fullbody.

Sanji smiled. "So today, all that's coming to a painful end!" Fast as lightning, the assistant chef placed his other hand on the floor and raised his legs into the air. Like a windmill, his legs spun around, slamming into the lieutenant. Fullbody flew across the room and slammed against the wall.

Zolo let go of his swords. It looked as if this assistant chef could handle himself quite well.

Sanji strode over to the lieutenant and picked him up by the neck. He raised Fullbody so high, his feet no longer touched the ground. "Don't forget," Sanji warned. "Offending a chef at sea is one mistake you should never make. Especially when that chef is I, Sanji!"

Suddenly a group of cooks ran down the stairs. "Sanji, no!" yelled one of the cooks.

"We've got to stop him!" shouted another.

A third cook stomped into the room. He was taller than the rest, making his white apron look as if he were wearing a large napkin. He didn't wear the white uniform that the other cooks wore. He wore giant boots, black shorts, and an orange scarf around his neck.

One of the other cooks grabbed his oversize forearms. "Look, Patty! We have to stop him!"

"That's a customer!" Patty cried. "Sanji, what

are you doing? How many times do I have to tell you, *the customer is always king*! Now show some respect!"

"Is that so, crud cook?" Sanji replied. "I think you better show me some respect!"

"Crud cook?!" Patty stomped over to Sanji. "Listen, you crud server! Customers are the lifeblood of a restaurant!"

Lieutenant Fullbody struggled to break free but Sanji continued to hold him off the ground.

"A customer?" asked Sanji. "First of all, this lowlife wasted precious food. And then he insulted the cooks." Sanji let go and the lieutenant fell in a heap. "So I *learned* him some etiquette."

Fullbody scrambled backward. "This place stinks! The food's full of bugs and the service is lousy." He raised a fist at Sanji. "I'll close you down! That's what I'll do. I have the authority. I'm a naval officer!"

"What?" asked Sanji. "Close the place down?" He marched toward the lieutenant. "Not if I close you down first!"

"Don't do it, Sanji," said Patty. He held him back.

"Who does that jerk think he is?" Sanji asked

65

as he struggled to break free. "Acting high-and-mighty. I can't stand ignorant slobs like him."

The other cooks quickly helped Patty restrain Sanji. "Hold on to him, boys," Patty ordered. "Don't let him go or that lieutenant's a goner for sure!"

Sanji inched closer to Fullbody. "I'm going to get you, Mr. Bigshot, got that?!"

CHAPTER THIRTEEN

Meanwhile, back upstairs, Luffy ducked just in time. Chef Zeff's peg leg swung mere inches over his head. Unfortunately, Luffy was so focused on the chef's leg that he didn't see the fist coming. He saw stars as he flew across the cabin once again. He smashed into an old wooden sea chest. Splinters exploded all around him.

The angry chef marched toward him and grabbed him by the leg. He lifted him off the ground and brought him to eye level. "What's it going to be, boy?" roared the chef. "A year of your life or this leg?" He gave Luffy a shake. "You have to choose one!"

"No, I don't!" yelled Luffy. With his free leg, he kicked the chef in the jaw. Zeff dropped Luffy before he flew back onto his bed. When he flopped onto the mattress, the bed legs crumbled beneath it.

Luffy didn't know what to do. He didn't want to work there for a whole year. Unfortunately, his *negotiation* with the chef was causing even more damage. If things kept going as they were, Luffy would have to work for Chef Zeff the rest of his life.

Zeff leaped off the bed. "Stubborn brat!" The floorboards creaked as he landed next to Luffy. He raised his peg leg once more. Luffy barely rolled out of the way before the peg smashed into the wooden floor. The planks below them cracked and, before he knew it, Luffy and the chef fell through the floor.

Luffy shook his head and climbed out from under the chef and broken planks. They were in a large dining room full of customers. Usopp, Zolo, and Nami were there as well.

Usopp pointed to the ceiling. "Look," he said. "They fell right through."

Luffy rubbed his head and looked at the jagged hole above him. "Whoa, that was different."

Suddenly, Chef Zeff grabbed Luffy's vest. "Curses! You broke my ceiling! It's all your fault, you brat!"

Luffy shook free. "What?! You jumped on me too hard!"

"Chef, you've got to help us stop Sanji," said a nearby voice. "We can't hold him much longer!"

"Huh?" said Zeff and Luffy.

Luffy saw that several cooks were restraining a man in a black suit. He was trying to get at that mean navy guy, Fullbody. The navy lieutenant sat amongst a pile of debris on the floor. From the looks of things, the guy called Sanji had already worked him over pretty well.

"Let me go!" yelled Sanji. "I'm not done with him yet!"

"Sanji!" Zeff boomed. "Are you attacking the clientele again?"

Sanji shot a look to the chef. "Zip it, old geezer!"

Zeff stomped toward Sanji. The other cooks

let go and backed off. "How dare you speak to me like that, you lolli-sucking loser!" The chef smacked him with his peg leg.

Lieutenant Fullbody laughed. "Well done!"

"Yeah?!" asked the chef. He swung his leg and smacked the navy lieutenant as well. Fullbody slid across the floor. "I've had enough of you too! Now be on your way!"

A tall, big-armed cook helped Sanji to his feet. "The customer is king," he said. "Got that, kid?"

Sanji dusted off his suit. "Yeah, I'll give anyone a crown who can eat your slop and survive!"

Chef Zeff rounded on them. "Sanji! Patty! If cooks are going to fight, they should do it in the kitchen!"

Suddenly, a navy crewman burst into the restaurant. "Lieutenant Fullbody!" He yelled. "I have an urgent message for you!"

Luffy shook his head. "Wow, this place is a madhouse."

The crewman shivered as he stood at attention in the doorway. "I'm afraid I have terrible news, Lieutenant!"

Fullbody stumbled to his feet. "Out with it!"

"Sir, that pirate from Krieg's crew escaped. He beat up seven of us and got away!"

"That's absurd!" the lieutenant barked. "The man was passed out from starvation when we captured him."

The restaurant patrons began to panic. "Krieg and his crew are near here?!" asked one of the customers.

"They're the toughest pirates in the eastern seas!" said another.

"Forgive me, sir," said the crewman. "I'm sorry that . . ." He suddenly flew forward and landed on his face. A lone figure stood silhouetted in the doorway behind him.

The customers stood and backed away from the entrance. "Pirates!" yelled a woman.

"Run for your lives!" yelled a man.

CHAPTER FOURTEEN

Everyone watched in fear as the lone man casually walked into the restaurant. He wore a thick headband and a jacket covered in snake designs. The man strolled to a large table and sat in a chair. He leaned back and placed his feet on the table.

"New customer," said the cook called Patty. "Party of one."

Zeff squinted at the man. "I've had my fill of trouble, so he better not try to bust up the place."

Wow! Luffy thought. *A real pirate!*

Patty stepped up to the table and smiled. "Welcome to Barbatie, squid man."

"Fetch me some food," ordered the pirate. "And don't keep me waiting. I'm real mean when I have to wait."

Patty leaned closer. "Pardon me, monsieur, but can you pay for this meal?"

Fullbody chuckled. "That cook's going to be roadkill."

The pirate slammed a fist on the table. "I'm only saying this once more, so listen. I'm a customer. Bring me food, now!"

Patty gave a wide grin. "You *don't* have any money, do you?" He raised both fists over his head. "Well, here's what I serve freeloaders!" The pirate leaped to the ground as the cook slammed his fists on the chair. Only a pile of kindling remained.

"Blast that Patty," grumbled Zeff. "He broke another chair!"

Whoa! thought Luffy. *He's strong!*

The entire restaurant cheered. Patty gave them

a wave, then leaned over the man. "If you can't pay for the cooking, then you ain't a customer!"

The pirate launched himself at Patty. The giant cook easily slammed him back to the ground. The crowd cheered louder.

"I've had enough of this," said Fullbody. He crawled toward the front door. "I'm leaving this rough-house!" The navy crewman crawled out after him.

Patty waved at the crowd again. "Thank you, dear customers!" He picked up the pirate and threw him over his shoulder. "Now please enjoy your meals."

Luffy followed Patty as he hauled the man out the front door. The cook heaved him over the railing and dumped him onto the lower deck. "Come again!" Patty yelled. He dusted off his hands and marched back inside.

Luffy leaned over the railing to get a better look at the pirate. "Are you all right down there?"

"Aye," he replied. "Why wouldn't I be?" The man tried to get up, then slumped back to the ground. "I'm just resting. I never felt better."

"What?" asked Luffy. "You look a little hungry to me."

The pirate rolled onto his back and glared up at Luffy. "Put a cork in it! I'm not the least bit hungry. Whatever gave you that idea?"

Luffy was about to offer him some limes from the *Merry Go*. After all, they sure helped Yosaku. But just then, the restaurant door opened. Sanji stepped out holding a tray of food. He walked down the stairs and set it in front of the pirate. Sanji then slumped against the rail and turned the lollipop over in his mouth.

"If you want to feel better, eat," Sanji suggested. "Fresh shrimp, tender calamari, sautéed together with garlic and onions in a nice oyster sauce."

Trembling, the man looked away from the steaming plate. "Stop it," he said. "I don't need your charity. I may have hit hard times, but I don't want your pity or your help."

Sanji looked out at the ocean. "Without food or water, this sea can be a pretty cruel mistress. I learned that the hard way."

Luffy could see the pirate's mouth watering from the upper deck. Why didn't he just eat?

"So if you want to starve, go ahead," said Sanji. "But I recommend that you swallow your pride along with that meal. That way, you'll live to see another day."

"Aye!" said the pirate. He crawled to the tray and began to eat. He shoved in spoonful after spoonful, ravishing the plate of food. Tears began to flow down his cheeks. "Better than I deserve," he said between bites. "I thought I was a goner. Done in by starvation." He shoveled more into his mouth. "I never tasted anything so delicious!"

Sanji beamed with pride. "Thanks. I made it myself."

It looks like I found him! thought Luffy. *I found my new head cook!*

Luffy leaned over the railing. "Hey, Mr. Cook! Want to join up with my crew?" asked Luffy. "You can be the cook for my pirate ship!"

"Huh?" Sanji looked up at him. "You're a pirate?"

"Yep!" Luffy swung over the railing and landed below. He sat on the deck next to the others.

"You don't look like much of a pirate," said Sanji. "And what kind of a pirate fires on an unarmed restaurant? That cannonball of yours almost sank the whole place."

Luffy cringed. "Sorry about that. It was self-defense, honest. I didn't mean to hit you."

"Self-defense?" asked Sanji. "Well, you better watch your step around here. Chef Zeff used to cook for a famous pirate. A very famous and dangerous pirate."

"Are you saying that old guy with the mustache is a pirate?" asked Luffy.

"That's right," replied Sanji. "This restaurant is the old ratbag's treasure. And all the cooks who flock to him are a bunch of hot-blooded pirate types too. With so many cutthroats passing through, they're the perfect crew for a joint like this."

"Yep," Luffy agreed. "It's a nuthouse, all right. I can see how someone would really enjoy working here. But you should come sail with me."

Sanji shook his head. "I'm afraid I have to decline. I just can't do it. I got my reasons for staying at this restaurant. You understand me?"

"No siree," said Luffy. "*I* decline!"

"What?" asked Sanji. "You decline what?"

Luffy hopped to his feet. "I decline your decline, okay? It's just that simple. I've made up my mind. You're a good cook and you're joining my crew!"

Sanji leaped to his feet as well. "Now hold on! You're not listening to me!"

"So, you're a pirate too," interrupted the man. "My name is Ghin. What are you doing here, kid?"

Luffy turned from Sanji and stood proudly. "I'm after One Piece, mister! So I'm on my way to the Grand Line!"

"The Grand Line?" asked Ghin. He shook his head. "If you don't even have a cook on board, you must not have much of a pirate crew on that ship of yours."

Luffy pointed to Sanji. "This guy makes five total."

"I told you, don't count me in!" Sanji bellowed.

"Whatever you do, matey, *don't* go to the Grand

Line." Ghin took off his headband and wrung out the sweat. "You're still young. Don't rush to your doom. There are plenty of safer waters to plunder than the Grand Line."

"What do you know about the Grand Line?" asked Luffy.

"Hardly anything," Ghin replied as he stood. He threw a leg across the railing and climbed into a small sailboat. "But what I do know scares me to the bone."

"No matter what, I'm still going to the Grand Line," said Luffy.

Ghin untied the mooring rope. "Do what you will. If you want to throw your life away, then it be none of my business." He looked up at Sanji. "And you, Sanji, my many thanks, matey. You saved my life with that meal of yours. That was the finest grub I've ever had. Can I come back and eat again?" asked Ghin.

Sanji gave a small bow. "Any time you like."

"There you are, chore boy!" Zeff's voice bellowed from above. The tall chef glared down at Luffy from the upper deck.

"Uh-oh," said Luffy.

The chef pointed at Ghin. "And what are you still doing here?"

Sanji waved Ghin away. "Don't worry about eating and running, just scram. And good luck."

Ghin hung his head. "I'm sorry. I bet I got you in real trouble. You'll surely be getting a lashing for giving me that free meal."

"I have no idea what you're talking about, Ghin, old boy," said Sanji. He stepped forward and kicked the dishes into the ocean. "A free meal? I don't see any free meals around here. Do you?"

As the boat drifted away from the restaurant, Ghin got on his knees and bowed before Sanji. "I won't forget my debt to you, Sanji. I won't forget!"

"Sanji! Chore boy!" Zeff bellowed. "Get to work!"

As Luffy followed Sanji into the restaurant, he glanced back at the pirate Ghin. The grateful man continued to bow on the deck of his tiny boat. He continued to pay his respect to Sanji.

CHAPTER FIFTEEN

Chef Zeff led Luffy to the upper deck and tossed an apron at him. "Your year of free labor starts now," he barked. "And since you don't know a thing about the restaurant business, you're Baratie's official chore boy."

Luffy had a friend once who was a chore boy, so he knew exactly what that meant. It meant he had to do *whatever* they told him, *whenever* they told him. Luffy also knew that it was no use arguing anymore with the chef. They would just get into another fight and tear up the place some more. He would have to come up with another way to repay his debt.

Luffy tied the apron around his waist and stepped into the kitchen. The long room was full of activity. Metal clanked and steam filled the air as cooks lined the prep area on one side and the stoves on the other. Everyone was chopping, mixing, frying, and sautéing. The hot air was filled with a cacophony of busy sounds and delicious odors.

Luffy put his hands on his hips. "The name's Luffy and I'm the new chore boy, reporting for duty!" he said proudly. "Nice to meet you!"

The cooks glanced over their shoulders then went back to work. Only Patty continued to glare at him. "If you got nothing to do, start washing dishes, chore boy!"

Luffy stepped up to a large metal sink stacked full of dirty plates, bowls, and silverware. He sighed as he began to fill the sink with soapy water. Washing dishes certainly wasn't in a pirate's job description. But until he could think of a way to repay his debt, he'd better get good at it.

Meanwhile, the rest of the cooks ignored him.

They went on with their conversations as if he weren't there.

"Did you hear about Sanji feeding that pirate fella?" one of the cooks asked.

"Aye," answered another.

"Well, I heard that he was one of Krieg's cut-throats!" said a cook with thin glasses and a beard.

"Yeah, he did say something like that," said Patty. He filleted a fish with expert precision. "What's it to you, Carne?"

"Don't you know that Don Krieg is the fierc-est, meanest pirate ever to unfurl a sail in these here waters?" Carne asked.

"That's right," agreed another cook.

A soapy plate slipped from Luffy's hand. *CRACK!* It shattered against the side of the sink. None of the cooks seemed to notice.

"Krieg is the Don of the Pirate Armada," Carne explained as he whisked a bowlful of eggs. "He com-mands over fifty bloodthirsty, battle-hardened pirate crews!"

Whoa! thought Luffy. *That's a lot of pirates!* Another plate slipped from his fingertips. *SMACK!*

"He's a monster," Carne continued. "A demon!"

"So what?" asked Patty as he filleted another fish. "Big whoop!"

Carne pointed a thin knife at Patty. "If that pirate fella tells Krieg how *you* treated him, they'll demolish us! They'll run over us like a heard of stampeding mad bull elephants!" Carne made chopping motions with his knife. "They'll chop us all into mincemeat and feed us to the fishes!"

"Bah!" Patty shook his head. "We're the ferocious fighting cooks. We got a reputation. We've chased off more pirates than the Royal Navy. If you're afraid of a few beggars and lowlifes, why don't you just turn in your hat and quit!"

"That's the same baloney you said to all our waiters," said Carne. "And you know what happened to them? They *all* quit!"

SMASH! Luffy dropped a bowl that time.

"Ha!" Patty chopped up another fish. "Those lily-livered fools were useless anyway! Good riddance!"

CRACK! Another plate.

"Chore boy!" Patty slammed down the knife and stomped over to him. "What are you doing? How many dishes have you broken here today?"

Luffy looked down at the sink full of broken plates and bowls. "Sorry, I forgot to keep count."

Patty turned off the faucet. "Okay, that's enough dishwashing, I mean dish breaking for one day." He handed Luffy a broom. "Clean up this floor. Then go bus the tables!"

"Okay," said Luffy. He began to sweep when he suddenly slipped on the slick floor. He reached out to catch his balance and grabbed a pot on the stove. "Ow! Hot!" He swung the broom around, knocking over a tall stack of dishes. *Ka-SMASH!*

"Get out of this kitchen!" Carne bellowed. "You're messing up everything!"

Patty jerked the broom from Luffy's hands and grabbed him by the face. "Just ask the customers what they like." With Luffy's feet dangling, Patty carried him out of the kitchen. "Do you think you can do that?"

Luffy nodded as best he could.

Patty dropped him to the floor. "And don't forget the customer is king."

"Got it," said Luffy.

Luffy rubbed his face as he walked down the stairs to the main dining area. Being a chore boy was harder than he thought. He had to think of a way to get out of this.

"Oh, chore boy!" sung a familiar voice.

Luffy spun around to see Nami, Usopp, and Zolo sitting around a large table. A large spread of fine food lay before them.

"So, you have to work here for a whole year?" asked Usopp.

Zolo laughed. "Should we change our flag to the Hungry Roger?"

Luffy ran up to the table. "You guys are eating without me?" he asked. "I'm slaving away in the kitchen and you're eating without me? That's just plain mean!"

"No, it's not," said Zolo. "Why can't we enjoy a nice meal out?"

Suddenly, Sanji appeared beside the table. "Oh, how grateful I am for this day of days!" He knelt beside Nami and held out a red rose.

"Huh?" she said.

"Yes, I would stoop to becoming a pirate or even a demon," Sanji continued. "If only I could be with you, my dearest petunia!"

Nami took the rose, then glanced at the others with confusion. Everyone merely shrugged their shoulders.

"Such epic tragedy!" Sanji stood and clutched his chest. "The obstacles between us are many and great!"

THUD! Chef Zeff's peg leg slammed onto the floor. "Who were you calling an obstacle, Sanji?"

Sanji sighed. "The old geezer."

"Well, now's your chance," said the chef. "Follow your heart while you're still young and go be a pirate." He stroked his braided mustache. "Go on! I don't need you here anymore. Adventure awaits you!"

A wide grin stretched across Luffy's face. Perhaps he could convince Sanji to join them after all — with the help of Nami. Of course, Luffy still couldn't leave until his year was up. There just had to be another way to pay back Chef Zeff. There just had to.

CHAPTER SIXTEEN

The sun was setting as Don Krieg's island hideout came into view. Ghin stood on the deck of his tiny boat and took it all in. The looming mass of jagged rocks certainly was a sight for sore eyes. Ghin smiled. It was good to be home.

However, as he sailed into the lagoon, he spotted a terrible sight. It was Don Krieg's flagship. The giant warship was a terrifying vision for most other people. But to Ghin, the ship was his home. Today, though, the sight of it filled him with despair — its